Crumble's Adventures

GW00578188

Mike Beale

Illustrated by
Maureen Fayle

First published in the UK 2015

Violet Circle Publishing.
Manchester, England, UK.

ISBN: 978-1-910299-06-7

www.violetcirclepublishing.co.uk

Introduction

This little book has been inspired by two mischievous and funny little dogs, Crumble and Alex. Crumble is a smooth-haired Jack Russell cross with a coat as black as soot with tan markings. Alex is a little bigger with a teddy bear face. She is wire-haired, with a brindle coat and a love of the outdoors.

Crumble was called Crumble because her Mum was called Apple. Alex was called Alex because the children in this story, Charlie and Ollie, call every soft toy and pet Alex.

Crumble and Alex are the very best of friends and play endlessly together. They like long walks but, best of all they like diving in and out of thickets and overgrown woods and chasing rabbits that they never catch.

Crumble is very sociable and wants to say hello to everyone she meets, and wags her tail furiously. She is a fantastic 'tracker' and her favourite pastime is eating. Alex is an outdoor girl and a little more aloof. She loves an adventure and would sooner get on with chasing squirrels and rabbits than sitting in front of a fire.

They live with Mrs Round in an old farmhouse called Pinkneys in a village called Westwood Green.

They both have big smiles and make people happy. And they hope this little book will make you happy as well!

Chapter 1

An Unexpected Visitor

"Clang," went the prison door. Two soft brown eyes looked up at PC Pipkin with large teardrops running down her face.

The little black and tan mongrel had arrived in the world and almost all at once had been separated from her Mum and Dad, brothers and sisters. With large floppy ears and a gentle face she looked very sad. She was tired from living rough and her coat was covered in dirt and grime. Her little ribs were sticking through her coat and she looked like a skeleton. With no home and no family the tiny smooth haired dog had managed to survive on scraps of food and the kindness of strangers.

1

Every day and every night the little dog
would wander the streets looking for food
and shelter and someone to care for her.
Little children would take pity on her and
give her a stroke and a biscuit if they had
one. But no one took her home with them.
And then her luck took a turn for the
worse. "What have we here?" Bellowed

PC Pipkin and the little dog shrunk into her skin. PC Pipkin was the village policeman in Westwood Green. Before she could make a move PC Pipkin had scooped her up and taken her back to his jail. Strays were not allowed on his patch.

That night the little dog cried and cried. She was feeling cold, lonely and unloved, and life seemed such a horrible thing. But what could she do? Everything was big and frightening, and she had no idea where she was.

The next morning PC Pipkin opened the cell door and threw some stale bread on the floor, together with a bowl of water. She was so hungry that she greedily ate the bread as fast as she could.

Day after day the same routine, stale bread and water, but gradually she grew stronger and a plan started to form in her mind. She would need to be brave and strong.

The very next morning she lay very still in her cell, hardly daring to breathe. When PC Pipkin opened the cell door he could not see any movement from the little stray and bent down to see what was wrong.

In a flash she jumped up, dashed through PC Pipkin's legs and was out of the cell, through the front door and into the street.

Without a backward glance, she ran and ran until her little legs could carry her no further and she collapsed in a large field of corn. Anxiously she looked around, but no one had followed her and for the moment she was safe. After all her adventures and the warmth of the sun, she fell asleep and dreamt of big bowls of food, warm beds and friends to play with.

Some hours later she woke with a start. There was a rustling noise nearby, and then a shrill fearsome bark that made her jump. She was very frightened and even more afraid of being taken back to PC Pipkin's prison.

The rustling noise got louder. There was someone or something crawling through the undergrowth and heading in her direction. Where to go? What to think? Before she could make a move a little teddybear-faced dog with a big smile poked her head through the corn and was nose to nose with the scruffy little stray.

"Hello, my name is Alex, who are you?"
Trembling, the little black and tan dog
replied, "I haven't got a name and I have
lost my Mum and Dad. I have no family or
friends, and I'm hungry and frightened."
Alex was a wire-haired terrier just a little
bigger than the stray. By nature she was a
kind and caring dog and took pity on this
little scrap.

"There's no need to be frightened any
longer. I will look after you. I live in a big
old farmhouse called Pinkneys with Mrs

Round. Let's get you home and safe," said Alex.

Alex took off at a fast trot with the little stray struggling to keep up. They ran and ran for what seemed like miles. Just when the little dog felt she couldn't take another step, they arrived at the kitchen door of a lovely old farmhouse. The scruffy little dog could not believe the heavenly smells coming from the kitchen. The aroma of warm bread, scones, meat pies and apple tarts was just too much. Her eyes watered and her stomach rumbled so much she nearly fainted.

A large round woman filled the doorway. She had a round head on a round body and her hair was rolled up into a round bun. She bent down to stroke the little dog, who immediately took fright and hid behind Alex for safety.

Mrs Round laughed, and said in her warm gentle voice, "now, now my love, what have we here? You look just about done in. You come here and rest up a minute. Are you hungry? Would you like something to eat?" The little black scrap couldn't believe her ears, something to eat! A large smile spread across her face and Mrs Round knew the answer. She waddled back indoors and soon the noise of singing together with the crashing and banging of pots and pans filled the air. And the most wonderful smells floated through the door.

A few minutes later Mrs Round emerged with a large bowl of steaming food. Ignoring her natural good manners the little dog launched herself at the small mountain of food. Happy sounds of slurping and crunching could be heard as she demolished the best meal in the whole world.

Just as she finished her first proper meal Mrs Round scooped up the little dog and announced, "you need a bath!" Thirty minutes later the scruffy, dirty little scrap had turned into a sleek and beautiful black and tan puppy with a glossy shiny coat. True, she was still very thin but a few more of Mrs Round's meals would soon change that.

Mrs Round turned to Alex, who had been sitting quietly watching all the proceedings. "Alex, you are such a good girl to find this little one, and bring her home safe to us." Turning to the little dog she said, "I've just finished cooking tonight's tea, we are having apple and blackberry crumble. I think we will call you Crumble."

Chapter 2

Crumble and Alex Go Caving

Crumble and Alex became good friends and spent each day playing and exploring. Alex being the older and wiser dog took charge and showed Crumble all her favourite haunts where they could chase rabbits and squirrels.

Alex and Mrs Round became her family and Pinkneys her home. Crumble knew how lucky she was. A lovely house, comfy bed, warm food and good friends. What more could a girl want?

Each day was filled with fun and adventure, and each day Crumble grew a little bigger and a little stronger.

Occasionally Crumble would think about her brothers and sisters and hoped that one day they would meet again and share their stories. Perhaps she might even find her Mum and Dad.

Alex was enjoying having a new friend and being able to teach her new tricks and ways to get extra treats. They were the best of friends.

One day Alex said. "Let's go down to the beach and explore the rocky coves. There are usually a few crabs to chase." Crumble could not wait.

Her adventures with Alex were always good fun and brought many surprises. Off they set across the fields and were soon scampering down the cliffs.

As Alex predicted, there were plenty of rocky pools and caves to explore and play in.

Crumble noticed a big hole in the cliffs
and asked Alex about it. "That's a very
big cave that leads to a secret cavern. Only
a very few people have ever been inside,
because it is so dangerous. It is said to
contain the treasure of Eric the Pirate."
Crumble had never heard of Eric the
Pirate and wanted to know more. Alex
continued, "Eric died about 100 years ago
and lived in the next village of Bracknell
Haven. He was the most famous smuggler

in the whole of England, and his partner in crime was a Frenchman known as La Petite Canard on account of his duck like walk. Together they would arrange to smuggle rum and brandy from France in exchange for guns and ammunition. They were also known to hijack ships when they got the chance and steal gold and jewellery."

Crumble was glad that Eric was no longer around. She took off with a call to Alex. "Race you there."

Alex in hot pursuit caught up with her little friend and together they raced into the cave. It was very dark and very damp, but very exciting. The cave soon divided into a number of different tunnels, and without thinking they dived down the one that looked the biggest. Soon they entered a huge cavern with more tunnels leading off it. Alex led the way. The tunnel started to get smaller and narrower, and soon they had to crawl along because the roof was so low. And then it happened, Alex called back to Crumble, "I'm stuck!" Poor Alex couldn't go forward and couldn't go back. She had got completely wedged.

Crumble was frightened but was determined to help her friend. She pushed and shoved as hard as she might, but could not get Alex to move even a tiny fraction of an inch. Together they must have tried for over an hour but still nothing. Alex was scared and started to cry, and Crumble knew she needed to get help.

Telling Alex her plan, Crumble quickly retraced her steps and had reached the big cavern with its many tunnels, when she heard the most terrible roaring noise, the tide was coming in, and the sea was starting to fill the cave. With each new crash of the waves, the water was getting higher and blocking the entrance. They were trapped, there was no way out and with every minute they were in further danger.

There was no alternative but to run back to Alex and try again. But in her haste and panic, Crumble took the wrong tunnel and was soon completely lost. More tunnels and more caves and yet none of them led back to Alex. Tired and frantic, Crumble kept running and calling to her friend.

All the while the roar of the sea got louder and louder and closer and closer. Then Crumble heard the faintest noise coming from somewhere to her left. There it was again, but just a little louder.

Without hesitation Crumble dived into the nearest tunnel where the sound came from. The water was now up to the top of Crumble's little legs and she knew that they were running out of time.

Alex's cries were now getting louder and Crumble knew she was getting close. Rounding a bend, she suddenly came face to face with Alex. Somehow Crumble had managed to go round in a circle.

Once Alex saw Crumble she stopped crying and had a big smile on her face. If anyone could save her, it was her best mate Crumble.

Crumble could now reach Alex's collar, and instead of pushing could now pull. Getting a good grip on her collar Crumble used all of her strength to try and pull Alex free. Once, twice, three times Crumble pulled, but Alex was stuck firm. The water had now reached their noses and they both knew it was hopeless, it was all over.

But Crumble was not done yet. She grabbed Alex's collar one last time and gave the most almighty heave, and with the sound of a cork coming out of a bottle, Alex was free. There was no time for thanks, and both girls took off as fast as they could through the cold and fear-some water.

They left the water behind them but they did not know where they were going; they just ran as fast as they could.

Eventually they came to another cavern they had never seen before with yet more tunnels leading from it.

Alex stopped and cocked her head to one side. She then sniffed the air. Crumble was puzzled. "Come on Alex, let's keep moving."

"Couldn't you feel it?" said Alex. "There is a draught of air. We must be close to one of the old air shafts, driven into the cliffs when they were looking for copper."

Following her nose and her instincts Alex took off with Crumble close behind. Each step took them further away from danger. They could start to feel the fresh air on their faces and soon they were clambering out of the old shaft and into the fresh air

Tongues out and panting heavily, they were on top of the cliffs with big smiles of relief. Alex turned to Crumble. "What a friend. You risked your life to save me and it was only because you are so strong that you could pull me free. I owe you a very big thank you."

Crumble smiled back at Alex. "Without your help I would still be a stray. You rescued me and brought me home, you're my best friend ever. I was never going to leave that cave without you."

Alex fought back a little tear. "Let's get home as soon as we can," said Alex. "Yes," said Crumble, "I'm hungry after all that adventure. We'll look for Eric's treasure another day."

Chapter 3

A Case of Mistaken Identity

Life on the farm with Mrs Round and Alex was wonderful, with plenty of fun and good dinners. Crumble missed her Mum, Dad, and brothers and sisters, but was so lucky to have found her new family. Alex took a lot of pleasure out of introducing Crumble to all her friends on the farm. There was Milly the donkey, who was quite old, but full of mischief. There were a lot of chickens who all got in a flap when Alex and Crumble were about, and with pigs, sheep and cows the farm was just full of friends to visit.

But their best friend was Harry the Horse. Harry was a beautiful horse, a dark chestnut brown with huge eyes and a wicked sense of humour.

Most days Harry, Alex and Crumble would get together and plan their adventures. They would often go miles and miles looking for new places to explore and just enjoy mucking about together. And they looked out for each other just to make sure no one hurt themselves or got into trouble.

The girls normally slept in the farmhouse in the old boot room, but when the weather was warm they would sleep with Harry in his stable. Endless summer days playing in the fields and woods, and trips to the beach to play in the waves were just the very best as far as Alex and Crumble were concerned.

It was the end of just such a summer's day when Alex and Crumble said goodnight to Harry and made their way back to Mrs Round and dinner. With full bellies they settled down in the old boot room and were soon snoring gently and dreaming of chasing rabbits.

In the middle of the night they heard a loud banging coming from the stables followed by a lot of neighing. It could only be Harry, he must be in trouble.

Alex and Crumble hurtled out of their room and raced across the farmyard and into the stables. There was Harry on his back legs, kicking and bucking. Three men had got ropes round Harry's neck and were trying to drag him into the back of their battered old horse box. Harry was having none of it and was fighting them with all his strength.

Alex and Crumble could see what was happening and immediately launched themselves at the wicked men who were trying to steal Harry. Snarling and growling they raced at the men, Harry saw his friends and knew he was not alone. It was a tough fight, Harry kicking and bucking and the girls barking and biting and the men hanging onto the ropes and using whips.

The battle raged until one of the ruffians launched a big kick on Crumble who flew into the air and landed badly. Lying still, Crumble was too badly injured to move. It was now just Alex and Harry against the three horse rustlers. With one last heave the men pushed Harry into the horse box.

Alex did not know what was best to do. Stay with Harry or go and look after Crumble. Crumble was Alex's best friend, but Harry was against three hard men and needed all the help he could get. Crumble was injured and she too needed help. In the end Alex dashed into the horse box and just made it in time as the door was about to close, and the lorry drive away.

Crumble lay still for several minutes without moving. With every bone and muscle aching she struggled to her feet and limped bravely back to the farmhouse to raise the alarm.

Harry was so relieved to have Alex with him that his spirits rose and instinctively he knew that together they could somehow manage to escape. "How's Crumble?" asked Harry concerned for his small black and tan friend. "Crumble took a bad kick," said Alex wishing that she could be with her, "but she's tough and brave and I know she will be okay."

The horse box drove for what seemed like miles and miles, bouncing all over the place, as the driver just wanted to get as far away from the farmhouse as fast as possible.

Meanwhile Crumble was barking as loud as she could to wake Mrs Round. But no one stirred in the dark house. Eventually Crumble saw an old tin bucket on top of some empty boxes and knew if she could knock over the boxes it would make a noise, a big noise. And it did! From out of the bedroom window Mrs Round called, "What's happening down there?" At once she saw Crumble was injured but also fretting about something and where was Alex? Mrs Round made her way down to the yard as quickly as possible.

Crumble led her to the empty stable where Mrs Round let out a huge scream "Argghhh!, they've taken my Harry."

Without wasting a second, a tearful Mrs Round got on the phone to PC Pipkin and explained what had happened. PC Pipkin reassured Mrs Round. "They won't have got far and a big horse box is easy to spot. I'm on my way."

As the lorry sped along Harry and Alex formed a plan and knew exactly what they were going to do. They just had to wait and be patient. Eventually the lorry crunched over some ground and came to a halt. Harry and Alex could hear the men talking and making their way to the back of the lorry. Harry and Alex were ready to make their escape.

As soon as the door was open a fraction Alex was through like a greyhound and bit the first leg she could see. The ruffian immediately let go of the door and started to hop around clutching his injured leg.

Harry saw his chance and crashed through the other door, pushing the next man sideways into the bushes. The last man saw what had happened to his mates and just took off running for all his worth.

Alex looked at Harry and they both smiled, they were free. But Harry was worried. "Where are we? We are lost, and miles from home." Alex smiled, "Crumble and I know this patch of countryside from our days of exploring. Follow me and we will be back home in time for breakfast." Excited by their adventure they set off with Harry at a trot and Alex running like the wind, and loving every minute of their freedom.

In no time Harry and Alex were back at Pinkneys and just in time to see PC Pipkin examining the crime scene. Mrs Round cheered when she saw Harry and Alex dashing into the yard. Despite her sore ribs, Crumble ran to greet her friends and welcome them home.

PC Pipkin said, "Thanks to Alex and Crumble we have arrested the villains. Your good work enabled us to start tracking the villains and just as we were about to make an arrest a small dog and a large horse came shooting out the back of the lorry going hell for leather. Two of the villains are in hospital, one with a big gash in his leg and the other with a broken nose and black eyes from a door hitting him."

A puzzled look suddenly appeared on PC Pipkin's face, "A couple of months ago a little black and tan dog, just like Crumble, did a runner from my jail. If I ever find that little devil she will be back in jail in no time!" Crumble slunk away and hid behind Mrs Round. Was she going back to jail? A big smile crossed PC Pipkin's face, "But I think we can safely say this is a case of mistaken identity!"

Chapter 4

What Will We Do About Jack?

The Hurdy Gurdy music told Alex and Crumble that the circus had come to their village, Westwood Green. Alex knew all about the circus, the animals, the funfair and all the noisy rides. Crumble had never been to a circus and couldn't quite believe what Alex was telling her.

"There are these huge animals called elephants who are as big as a house, and tigers with really big teeth that look like Tom the Tabby but 20 times his size." Crumble couldn't imagine an animal larger than Harry the Horse, but if Alex said so it must be true.

"And they have this fairground with lots of games and music and everyone having fun," continued Alex. It sounded OK to Crumble but when Alex went on, "They also have BBQ stalls, and candy floss and lots of scrummy things to eat," that was when Crumble really took an interest. Crumble was a girl with an appetite.

They trotted over to the village green where they saw men putting up the big tent and getting the rides organised. They wandered round the fairground and saw the hoopla stand, and the penny machines and where the food stalls were being set up. So much noise and bustle, and it was all very exciting.

Their path home took them behind the big lorries that had brought the circus to the village. There they saw animals tied up and some in cages, all looking tired and unhappy. Alex and Crumble stopped to talk to some of them and hear about their life on the road, it didn't seem at all like their own happy lives.

They then spotted a little white and brown dog, sitting all alone in a cage with iron bars and hardly any room to move. Crumble remembered her own spell in prison and those iron bars and she shivered.

"Can you help me?" Alex and Crumble jumped with surprise that the little dog had spoken to them. Alex spoke first. "My name is Alex and this is my best friend Crumble. What's your name?"

"My name is Jack, silly name for a Jack Russell really."

"How can we help?" said Crumble. Jack replied, "I'm locked in this tiny cage every day and I never go out to play and have fun. Every evening I have to perform tricks because they know I'm clever, and can make the audience clap and cheer. I want to be free and have some real friends I can run and play with."

Alex and Crumble were devastated and realised what an unhappy life little Jack led. "Will you help me escape?" Alex and Crumble didn't hesitate. "Yes of course. How long will the circus be in the village?"

"We're here for three days and nights," said Jack and then we move to the next village. "Right," said Crumble, "we can't be seen to be hanging round here talking to you now. We will go home and work out a plan and come and see you at the same time tomorrow."

That evening Alex and Crumble worked on their plan. First of all they would need to know all Jack's movements throughout the day and evening. Hopefully they could spot an opening in Jack's handler's routines that they could take advantage of. That first night they watched Jack being brought into the ring and perform his fantastic tricks, balancing a ball on his nose, playing a drum and dancing, just amazing.

At the end of the performance Jack's handler, a fearsome man named Ivan, put him on a lead and took him out of the ring and straight back to his cage. Not for one second was Jack out of sight or not on his lead. This was going to be really tricky.

The next day Alex and Crumble went to Jack and explained the problem. With only two more nights to go they were running out of time. The second night was no different and Jack and the girls needed to come up with a plan quickly.

On the third day they all met again. They thrashed around some ideas but nothing seemed to work until Crumble shouted. "Got It! We need a diversion." They crowded round to discuss Crumble's idea and they all agreed it was their only chance, but full of risk. There was a danger that they might all get caught and end up performing with Jack in the circus.

That last evening Jack did his usual array of tricks, and the audience all stood to applaud and cheer his performance. Ivan emerged from the side of the ring with Jack's lead, ready to take him back to his cage.

At that very moment Alex and Crumble
raced into the middle of the ring barking
and running wild and causing chaos and
confusion. Jack joined in and so did the
other animals that were in the ring.

The elephants were trumpeting, the
horses neighing and the tigers roaring.
Clowns were running around and falling
over which only added to the fun and
confusion. In amongst all this chaos Ivan
lost sight of Jack, and Alex saw their
chance to escape. Calling to her friends

Alex raced out of the ring with Jack and Crumble close behind. Ivan just caught a glimpse of three little dogs hurtling out of the Big Tent, and set off in hot pursuit and desperate to catch them. But they were far too quick for Ivan and in no time they were free and running for home.

They had taken a risk and it had paid off. "What have we got here?" said Mrs Round when all three turned up late at night in her kitchen.

"Why, this looks like the little chap I saw last night in the circus. What's this little chap doing here?" The girls barked wildly and Mrs Round had her answer. "You've helped little Jack escape and brought him home. Well then we had better keep him hidden till the circus leaves the village." More barking and even Jack joined in.

Around midnight there was a loud banging on Mrs Round's front door, and a man shouted up at the house, "Have you seen a little white dog? He's been seen with two other dogs heading this way." It was Ivan. Alex, Crumble and Jack kept very quiet.

Leaning out of her bedroom window Mrs Round called back, "Haven't seen a dog of that description, but if I do I will let you know." The man left with a scowl.

Alex and Crumble were taken aback, Mrs Round had been untruthful! Sensing their concern, Mrs Round told the girls, "I haven't seen a little white dog. I've only seen a little white and brown dog." Alex and Crumble smiled, good old Mrs Round.

But they now had a different worry. Crumble spoke for both of them. "Mrs Round cannot afford to keep all of us. What will we do about Jack?"

Chapter 5

The Three Amigos

Jack fitted in perfectly with his new friends and surroundings. Alex and Crumble showed Jack around the farm and introduced him to all their friends, including Harry the Horse who took a particular shine to Jack.

In time Jack showed Alex and Crumble some of his tricks and taught them how to walk backwards whilst balancing on their back legs.

Jack could still remember his days in the circus, and trembled with fear when he remembered his life behind bars in a tiny cage. He was so grateful to his new best friends. They often talked about the great escape and how it seemed so scary, but now it seemed exciting and fun.

But they were all worried. Mrs Round was the kindest hearted person, but could not afford to keep all three of them, she didn't have enough money to feed them all. "Sorry my little ones, but one of you will have to go. As much as I love you all I cannot afford to keep the three of you!"

This made them all sad as Jack had quickly become one of the family, and life without him around seemed unthinkable.

Westwood Green's village fete was going to be soon upon them and everyone was making plans. They were hoping to raise enough money to repair the roof of the scout hut. The women were making jams and cakes and the men preparing the stalls. Everything from a tombola to a coconut shy to a merry go round.

At this time every year the vicar would call on Mrs Round to ask for her support and enquire what she might contribute to the fete. "Now, Mrs Round, what will you be providing for the fete?" said Father Murphy. "Oh dear me," replied Mrs Round, "I just don't know what we can do to help. Things are very tight and I have no money to spare." They talked for a little while longer, but in the end Mrs Round shook her head and said she would have loved to help, but this year was out of the question.

Jack and the girls heard this conversation and immediately started to come up with ideas of how they could help. It was Jack who came up with the best idea. "Why don't we put on a show? I can teach you all my tricks and together we can put on a show for all the villagers."

Alex and Crumble jumped at the idea and they immediately started to plan their show and rehearse their parts. Jack was a good teacher and soon they were all juggling balls, walking on tip toes and playing their own version of football. After some practice they went to see Mrs Round and show her their act.

"Well I never," said Mrs Round when she saw the show. They were pleased and all sat down in front of her and barked. She got the message, "You want to do your act at the fete? Well, I'll ask Father Murphy."

At tea the next day Father Murphy saw the friends put on their performance and laughed and clapped. "What a wonderful act," he said. "I am going to put you into the programme."

The girls and Jack were delighted and rehearsed and rehearsed until they got their routine perfect. Notices were put on trees and leaflets dropped through letter boxes advertising the fete and in particular the performance of the 'Three Amigos'.

It was just such a notice pinned to a tree that caught the eye of Ivan, the dog handler from the circus. Three dogs? Ivan remembered the chaos caused by Alex and

Crumble and how they escaped with Jack. This was his chance to get them back, and grab the lot of them. His dog act would soon be even better. Not just one dog, but three dogs all performing their tricks. He smiled an evil smile.

The day of the fete arrived and hundreds of people came to the village. Ice cream vans, BBQ stalls, tombola and skittles were all busy with happy visitors enjoying the day.

The big moment had arrived. Father Murphy with the help of some friends had created a little stage made up of big straw bales. When 3 o'clock came the crowds gathered round. At a signal from Mrs Round, Jack, Alex and Crumble all jumped onto the stage and began their act.

The crowd roared their approval and cheered them on as they played football,

danced and balanced balls on their noses
and walked backwards on tiptoe.

Everyone cheered and threw their
money into the collecting boxes. A voice
shouted "once more," and the Three
Amigos once again went into their routine.

After the show the three gathered back
stage to chat about this new adventure.
Before anyone could say anything a large
net was thrown over them. The next thing
they knew was being loaded into the back
of a van and being driven away.

Jack knew what had happened and
somewhat sadly told his friends, "We
have been captured and will now have to
spend the rest of our lives in the circus."
They couldn't believe their bad luck. They
were only trying to help raise funds for
the village and now they were prisoners.

What they didn't know was that Father
Murphy had spotted what had happened
and immediately told PC Pipkin. PC
Pipkin jumped onto his motorbike and
gave chase.

But Ivan had a head start, and as soon
as he got back to the circus unloaded the

friends and hid them away.

When PC Pipkin reached the circus he immediately accosted Ivan and demanded the return of Jack and the girls. Ivan was belligerent. "Don't know what you are talking about. There are no dogs round here."

Jack and the girls had heard PC Pipkin's voice and immediately started barking and howling for all they were worth. PC Pipkin took one look at Ivan and said, "I'm arresting you on the charge of dognapping. You will be going to jail for a long time." Ivan knew he was in deep trouble.

"Jack is my dog, but if you drop the charges I am happy to let him go to a good home." PC Pipkin thought this was a good solution and made Ivan promise to never ever again try and dognap Jack or either of his two friends.

Back in the village Father Murphy was delighted to see Alex, Crumble and Jack back home again. "You three have made this the most successful fete ever, and with the £100 from your performance alone we will be able to put a new roof on the Scout Hut." They were all pleased, but there was more good news.

"I have talked with Mrs Round and she has agreed that I can adopt Jack. He will come to live with me in the vicarage, which means you can play together whenever you want."

Jack, Alex and Crumble all looked at each other and furiously wagged their tails. Jack was free of the circus and would be part of their gang.

Crumble spoke for all of them, "I enjoyed putting on our performance, but once is enough!"

Chapter 6

Never Going to Lose My Best Friend

Alex loved being with Crumble and her other friends, but sometimes she liked going for a quick explore on her own.

The best times were early morning when no one was around, and she could venture far and wide with no one to disturb her. The whole countryside was her territory, from the cliffs and sea to the fields and woods beyond the farmhouse.

Alex never took the same route, always choosing to explore new smells and new paths. In the early morning she could often startle a rabbit or two and give chase. Being on her own meant she did not

have to look after her best friend,
Crumble, who was not quite so wise in the
ways of the countryside. Crumble loved
being with Alex, but was equally happy
to relax on a nice soft cushion in front of a
warm fire.

Alex, being slightly older felt
responsible for Crumble and would look
after her. Crumble was terribly inquisitive
and could easily get into trouble.

One day Alex woke early, and whilst
no one was around decided it was just the
kind of morning to go exploring. Alex set
off and went first to the cliffs and
wandered along the coast path. The cliffs
were covered with gorse and heather, and
were ideal territory for rabbits, squirrels
and mice. Alex was a hunter by nature,
and tracking down these creatures was
just part of her natural instincts. There was
nothing doing here, but the day was fresh
and young and there was plenty more
exploring to do.

Alex retraced her steps, crossed behind the farmhouse and entered the woods. They were more interesting than the cliffs, as there were so many more hiding places. There was also a lovely stream that cascaded over rocks and down little waterfalls. The water was always fresh and clean and to Alex the tastiest. She liked being in the stream and decided it was easier to use than trying to negotiate the overgrown woods.

There was an area in the middle of the

woods she had never explored and now seemed like a good time. This was an area with dense undergrowth, ferns, brambles, and dead trees that had fallen over and now provided a home for lots of insects and creepy crawlies. No doubt there was good hunting here.

Just inching her way through the dense undergrowth she started to pick up the scent of rabbit. Crouching low Alex started to carefully move forward. Suddenly there was a loud noise. "Grrrrr." And without warning Alex was set upon by two wild dogs. Inadvertently she had stumbled into their territory.

These were big savage dogs, who lived in the woods and had learned how to fight. Alex was good in a scrap and could usually look after herself, but she was outnumbered and these savages were determined to teach Alex a lesson.

The battle was intense with lots of barking, snarling and biting. Alex fought bravely and got in some good bites, causing one brute to let out a yelp of pain. The other dog bit deep into Alex's back leg. Alex grabbed this dog by the neck and clung on. The first dog had recovered and lunged at Alex. The noise of the fight reached fever pitch as the pain and anger mixed with the intensity of the barking and growling.

Alex launched another attack and bit the ear of one of them. Letting out a piercing scream the dog ran away. The other dog, sensing that Alex was too strong, and too brave, was not going to hang around, and immediately took off.

Cut and bleeding and badly hurt, Alex had seen off the wild dogs, but was now too injured to make her way home. She needed rest and time to recover, Alex limped away and sought shelter in a hidden part of the forest where the trees and bushes kept strangers away.

Back at Pinkneys, Crumble woke to find her friend missing. This was nothing unusual and she went off to find Mrs Round and get some breakfast organised.

"I've got a nice piece of bacon for you, and cold sausage," said Mrs Round. Crumble's eyes watered and her stomach rumbled. Eating was her favourite pastime and a good breakfast would set her up for the day. "And where's that scallywag Alex, out hunting again I expect?" She said with a smile in her voice.

The day wore on and Crumble became worried that Alex had not returned. When she went on these hunting trips she was usually back around mid-morning for a bite to eat. But no worry, Alex would turn up soon.

Lunch time came and went, and Crumble tucked into a nice beef stew, one of her many favourites. But, still no sign of Alex. Both Mrs Round and Crumble were now getting worried.

It was approaching tea time when Crumble decided enough was enough, and she needed to go and look for Alex. After taking a small snack to keep her going Crumble set off. Alex's scent was all over the farm, but Crumble having a really good nose was able to detect a fresh scent leading to the cliffs and took off at a pace. Almost following in Alex's every footstep Crumble was able to tell that Alex had doubled back and headed for the woods.

Crumble liked tracking, and all was going well until the trail led to the stream. Crumble realised that Alex must have entered the stream but once in the water the scent disappeared. Without a scent Crumble had to use guess work to try and locate where Alex had gone. Searching on both sides of the bank Crumble with her nose close to the ground carefully sniffed for a trace of Alex. This was slow and painstaking work but there was no alternative. It was now starting to get dark, and Crumble was worried that Alex must be injured and time was running out.

Crumble's scenting skills were the best, and she now picked up the faintest trace of where Alex left the stream. But worryingly she also picked up the smell of blood. Ignoring the signs of danger Crumble raced along the track where the scent of blood became stronger. Breaking through a dense copse of trees and gorse she found Alex lying on her side.

Alex raised her head a little and flickered a brief smile at Crumble and said. "Dear Crumble thank you for finding me, I know it could not have been easy." Alex went on. "But I'm too injured to walk." Crumble with tears in her eyes realised how badly hurt Alex was, and that urgent help was needed, but it might already be too late to save her best friend.

Crumble summoned up her courage and didn't want to let her friend know how serious this looked. "You are going to be OK. I'll run back and get help. Just stay there and rest." Crumble had never run so fast, and in no time was back with Mrs Round and barking wildly.

Mrs Round knew immediately what was wrong and what needed to be done. "I'm going to call Mr Victor the local vet, and you can lead him to Alex." Mr Victor got to Pinkneys as fast as he could. He had known Crumble since she was a puppy and knew she was to be trusted.

Picking up his medicine bag Mr Victor spoke to Crumble. "Lead on and take me to Alex." Mr Victor ran as fast as he could but could not keep up with Crumble. Every time Crumble had to stop to let Mr Victor catch up, she knew it was wasting precious time. When they got to the stream Mr Victor jumped in and got his shoes and trousers wet. Crumble knew exactly where to find Alex, and as they got closer they could hear a faint whimpering and ran even faster. Crashing through the dense barrier of bushes, Mr Victor saw Alex. Her wound and injuries were serious and she had lost a lot of blood.

Kneeling down beside Alex, Mr Victor got to work cleaning and bandaging the wounds. He then injected Alex with antibiotics to prevent infection. Speaking quietly to Crumble Mr Victor said, "she is very weak, but luckily there are no broken bones."

Mr Victor put Alex in a kind of stretcher that was part of a back pack specially made to carry injured animals. Alex hardly moved throughout their trek back to the farmhouse and Mrs Round.

"Make certain Alex is kept quiet and if she will eat, give her a little well-cooked steak," said Mr Victor. Crumble was disappointed to learn it was only Alex getting the steak.

"Alex may need to go to hospital, but for the moment she is better off here where you can give her lots more attention. I will call first thing tomorrow to check how she is doing."

Alex did not eat and just lay still. Crumble was worried and cuddled up to her best friend. Crumble waited till Alex had gone to sleep before she went into her own fitful sleep. They lay together all night with Crumble not daring to move.

As promised Mr Victor called first thing and checked on Alex's wounds and they seemed to be healing. He gave Mrs Round some more medicine and said. "Alex is making progress, but it will take time. There is no need to go to hospital, she just needs the comfort of home and her friends around her, particularly Crumble."

Later that day Alex sat up and had something to eat and managed to smile at Crumble. "Thanks Crumble, I think you saved my life. You are the best tracker around and the only one who could have found me. I would probably have been a goner."

Crumble smiled, "Don't be daft. You are as tough as old boots, besides I was never going to lose my best friend!"

Chapter 7

What Was in the Box?

"Charlie and Ollie are coming to spend their summer holidays with us," announced Mrs Round to Alex and Crumble. Alex was delighted and Crumble puzzled. Alex explained, "Charlie and Ollie are Mrs Round's grandsons and are great fun. They want to play games and go on treasure hunts and have lots of fun. And they will want us with them all the time so we can share their adventures." Crumble had never met Charlie and Ollie, but this sounded like fun.

Charlie was eight, a couple of years older than Ollie. Later that week the two boys arrived with big suitcase, footballs and cricket bats. The first thing they did was go and look for the girls to say hello. "Alex, Crumble!" They both shouted as they ran into the field behind Pinkneys.

The girls were exploring in the woods for rabbits when they heard the boys calling, and immediately raced to find them. The boys and the girls all collapsed together in a big heap of shouting and barking.

The first few days of the holiday were

fairly quiet as they explored the cliffs and the woods and generally messed around. Charlie and Ollie, as he was normally called, came up with a great idea and went to find Mrs Round.

"Can we go camping?" They both asked, "and stay out all night?" Mrs Round smiled. "Yes of course, providing you are not too far from the farmhouse and you take Alex and Crumble with you."

That day, the boys started to make their plans of where they were going to camp and what supplies they should have. Charlie volunteered to be the cook and started to list all the things he would need to take. "We will have chocolate, biscuits and lemonade, and lots of sweets." Ollie thought this was a good plan and suggested that they might also include cake.

Ollie then thought of the girls. "We will

need extra supplies for the girls, you know how they like cake and biscuits, particularly Crumble." Mrs Round helped them pack their back packs and included some essential items like sandwiches and water.

Early next morning they set off for their camp site. It was on the edge of the wood, and near the little stream. Alex and Crumble could not stop smiling and laughing. This was a great adventure and it was going to be a lot of fun. They loved nothing more than being with Charlie and Ollie and joining in all their games. But they also knew their job was to protect the boys, and make sure that they didn't come to any harm.

By mid-morning they had set up camp and eaten all the biscuits, largely with the help of Crumble. The two man tent was perfect, Alex and Crumble in one side and Charlie and Ollie in the other. After lunch of cake and lemonade the boys decided to explore the woods using Alex and Crumble as tracker dogs. The girls raced into the woods with the boys in hot pursuit. They ran through the trees and over the hills and into the valleys.

The day went so quickly and everyone had fun. By early evening the boys had lit a camp fire and were cooking some sausages that they had spiked on long sticks. Crumble and Alex licked their lips in anticipation and were not disappointed.

Settling down after their camp fire dinner Charlie suggested they visit the old church that used to be the centre of the village and was now derelict and overgrown with trees and shrubs.

Charlie and Ollie both had torches and set out through the woods. For Crumble and Alex this was exciting, but they didn't need torches as they could see perfectly well in the dark. They reached the old church which seemed eerie in the moonlight.

Both Alex and Crumble were very wary and did not want to go near the building and kept hanging back. The girls sensed evil spirits surrounding the church and graveyard and would have preferred to be back in their camp site by a warm fire.

As Charlie and Ollie approached they saw a flickering light inside the church.

Someone or something was moving
around. They were both very frightened
and Ollie, almost in tears said, "I'm

frightened. Let's go home." Charlie was frightened too, but didn't want Ollie to know. "Come on let's take a quick look through that side window."

Very quietly they worked their way round to the side of the church and looked in. Through the candlelight they saw the silhouette of a man using some sort of lever to lift one of the big flagstones on the floor.

Charlie turned and whispered to Ollie, "I bet he's up to no good. He must be looking for buried treasure." Ollie was no longer frightened. "We have to get PC Pipkin, but he is miles away."

Charlie had an idea, "I'll write a note and attach it to Alex's collar. Alex and Crumble can then run and fetch PC Pipkin."

Using an old chocolate wrapper that he found in his pocket, and the stub of a pencil, Charlie wrote a quick note and sent

Alex and Crumble on their journey with
the words. "Find PC Pipkin."

The girls were terribly excited and
realised they were on an important
mission. They ran like the wind and found
PC Pipkin just turning in for the night.

"Hello girls, what are you up to?" PC

Pipkin had got to know the girls and knew that this had to be important for them to stop him going to bed. He read the note and jumped onto his motorbike. "Lead on girls, and I will try and keep up." Alex and Crumble wanted to get back to the boys as soon as possible, so they raced through the woods as fast as they could.

Back at the church the thief was just removing an old wooden box from underneath the floor, and chuckling to himself. "At last the treasure is mine, all mine." Without hesitating he threw the box into his bag and made for the door. Charlie and Ollie kept hidden.

As soon as he was out of the church the villain started to head for the road where he had left his getaway car. The box was large and heavy, and the villain's progress was slow. Charlie and Ollie decided to follow him and just hoped that Crumble and Alex could pick up their tracks.

Alex and Crumble, with PC Pipkin just behind, soon reached the church and quickly realised that the boys and the villain had already left. But Crumble knew instantly which direction they had taken and set off at a furious pace. She was worried that the boys could be in trouble if the scoundrel had caught them and taken them with him.

Charlie and Ollie were closing on the thief when they saw him heave the box into the back of his car. Shouting, "stop thief!" The boys reached the car as the villain was about to drive off. He turned to see where all the noise had come from and set his evil eyes on Charlie and Ollie. His face was contorted with rage and hatred, and with a swift movement he leapt out of the car to face the boys.

By this time Alex and Crumble had just reached the road and saw the rogue about to raise his arm and strike out at Charlie and Ollie. "Let's go," shouted Alex to Crumble and they took off like rockets. Before the thief could move another inch Alex and Crumble had brought him down. Barking and snarling they pinned him to the ground. Charlie and Ollie sat on a leg each.

Going as fast as he could PC Pipkin soon arrived, and took control of the situation. "You are under arrest for the unauthorised removal of property from the old church, and you are now coming with me." Charlie and Ollie were safe and the girls had saved the day.

Charlie, Ollie, Crumble and Alex returned to their camp site excited and very tired and chatted about their adventures. A little while later the boys slipped into a deep sleep. Crumble turned to Alex and asked, "I wonder what was in the box?"

Chapter 8

The Dog and Pony Show

It was the last week of Charlie and Ollie's summer holidays and they had had a most wonderful time. Picnics, games, camping, and as always, with Alex and Crumble alongside them. Charlie had christened them, 'Our Girls'.

It was also the week of the Westwood Green Dog and Pony show. Alex had to explain to Crumble what this was all about. "We get to play lots of games with other dogs. We have races, an obstacle course, obedience classes and best in show. The ponies are great fun and take children for rides."

Crumble wanted to know if there was going to be food available, as when the village held the summer fete. Alex smiled, "dear Crumble, you have a one track mind. Yes, there will be BBQ stalls and candy floss stalls and cakes by the thousand." Crumble was delighted. This was her kind of event.

Charlie was taking this more seriously. "Mrs Round will want us to join in and enter 'Our Girls' in the obstacle race. Colin the Collie from Cookham is the current champion and is favourite to win. There is also Barney from Bourne End who is very quick. We will have to work hard if we are to stand a chance of winning for Westwood Green." Ollie suddenly piped up, "let's build Alex and Crumble an obstacle course and get in some practice."

Charlie and Ollie set to immediately and built jumps, created ramps, made tunnels and a special fence that the girls had to weave in and out of. There was also a big hoop to jump through and a water splash. The girls were very excited and were keen to get in some practice.

The day before the show Mrs Round called in the gang for tea. She had prepared scones with jam and cream, cakes and a big chocolate log. There were sandwiches and lemonade and a big bowl of crisps, a real feast.

"You boys and girls have been working really hard! And deserve to win some prizes. But there is some really exciting news. There is a whisper going round that a big celebrity will be coming to open the Dog and Pony show and judge some of the events."

The gang were really excited and wondered who it might be. Crumble thought it might be David Beckham and Alex suggested David Cameron. Charlie hoped it would be One Direction and Ollie thought it might be Beyoncé.

On the big day everything was ready, and Westwood Green looked a treat with coloured stalls, flags flying and lots of bunting everywhere. Charlie and Ollie had done a good job training the girls and both Alex and Crumble felt on good form.

By the time 2 O'clock arrived, the Green was packed with villagers and visitors and everyone was getting excited to see who the big celebrity was going to be.

A huge 'oooh' went up as a large black car with a crest on the roof pulled onto the Green. For a moment there was a stunned silence, and then a huge cheer, it was The Queen.

Smiling and waving to the crowd she opened the Dog and Pony show and took her place to watch the events. The ponies were on first and very much impressed Her Majesty with their routines. Next came a series of events for dogs including best looking and most waggly tail.

Alex and Crumble were saving themselves for the main event, the all-comers obstacle race. The course was set up just as Charlie and Ollie had predicted, and the girls were very excited.

A lovely golden retriever went first, followed by a black Labrador. Colin the Collie went next and set the best time of all. Jack, their best friend went next. Jack was lightning quick and tackled every obstacle with speed and agility, not putting a foot wrong. Alex looked a bit glum. "Both Jack and Colin have put in good times and no penalty points. We will have to run faster than we have ever run before." Alex and Crumble were the last to go. Alex went first and shot round the course jumping through hoops and dashing through tunnels and over jumps. She raced to the finishing line and set the best time of anyone. The whole crowd cheered. Alex was winning for the village.

Crumble knew she was faster than Alex, but not quite so agile, and would have to take care not to knock something over. Crumble took off like a rocket, and was leading at the half way point by a couple of seconds.

Alex was cheering her friend on and the crowd were clapping and shouting. Even the Queen stood up to cheer. Into the last bend, and Crumble took the most fantastic leap to clear the hurdle and cross the finishing line.

The crowd went wild with cheering. But something was wrong. All the judges had gathered together and were consulting their watches and clipboards. Much shaking of heads and tut-tutting went on and the crowd fell silent. What was wrong? The Queen was handed a piece of paper and she looked somewhat puzzled but then announced. "Both Alex and Crumble had clear rounds and achieved exactly the same time. After much deliberation the judges cannot separate them and have declared a dead heat. The winners are Alex and Crumble." The girls had won, and they were beside themselves with joy. They had won for Mrs Round and their village.

The Queen presented the prizes to all the winners, and when she came to Mrs Round and the boys she had a special word. "What beautiful dogs. And you two boys have trained them well. I have just lost one of my beloved corgis and I am looking to replace her. Would either Crumble or Alex like to train to be a Royal Corgi?"

Chapter 9

A Royal Summons

Alex slunk away. A corgi? Who would want to be a Royal Corgi? No chasing rabbits, early morning walks along the cliffs and in the woods. Freedom to come and go, and play with your mates. The life of a corgi was not for Alex.

Crumble could see the advantages. Lovely big houses that were always warm, and lots of servants to do all the chores. She would have her own room and her own footman to make sure she had everything she needed. And Crumble would meet lots of famous people and go lots of places. Plus three square meals a day, it couldn't be bad.

Mrs Round was honoured to think that The Queen would consider her two girls good enough to become Royal Dogs. It became the talk of Westwood Green. But Mrs Round did not want to lose her girls and was in a complete state as to what to do.

A few days later Mrs Round received a letter from The Queen, asking whether she had considered the request. Mrs Round was now in an even bigger dither as to what to do. She decided to ask Father Murphy round for tea and seek his advice.

"Well, Mrs Round. I have to say that such a request from The Queen is a real honour, and I feel you must do your duty by Her Majesty."

"But Alex would hate it. She is a real country girl and loves the open spaces. Being at that big house in London would not suit her at all." Said Mrs Round. "And what about Crumble?" asked Father Murphy.

Crumble was wildly wagging her tail. "Oh, I have no doubt that little Crumble would love all the cosseting, plentiful food and special treats. She already has a royal bearing and charming manners," said Mrs Round.

Father Murphy had the answer. "You will have to politely tell The Queen that Alex is not suitable and that Crumble will be willing to do her duty as a Royal Corgi." The matter was settled and a letter sent to The Queen.

A few days later the Royal car arrived in the village to collect Crumble. It was the same black car with the crest on the roof. Mrs Round had gathered up all of Crumbles toys, her favourite cuddly monkey and all her other belongings ready to load into the car.

A very smart footman knocked on the door and announced he was here to collect Crumble. "Very good," said Mrs Round. "I'll just go and get her and all her belongings."

"That won't be necessary," said the footman. "Crumble is all I have come for. She will be given a completely new wardrobe of collars and coats and a new set of toys."

"What about all her favourite toys and the cuddly monkey. She loves the cuddly monkey…" said Mrs Round. It was no use; the footman was adamant.

Crumble's excitement for this new adventure was rapidly disappearing. Not her own bed and not her favourite toys. And it all suddenly hit home. No Mrs Round. No fields to play in. And no playing with her best friend Alex.

Crumble turned to Alex with tears in her eyes. "Goodbye dear friend, I'm afraid this is the last time we will meet. You have been the very best friend I could have ever had. I will think of you every day and miss you every day."

Alex was sobbing uncontrollably, "Dear, dear Crumble, you go and have a most wonderful time. You will make new friends and I'm sure you will become the Queen's favourite. Perhaps you might even come to visit us some day."
Everyone except the footman was crying, Mrs Round, Alex and Crumble.

The footman put Crumble on to the rear seat, where there was a huge cushion.

Ignoring the cushion Crumble jumped up on to the rear parcel shelf and looked out of the back window as Mrs Round, Alex and the farmhouse disappeared from view.

Crumble could not feel more desolate and cried all the way to Buckingham Palace.

On arrival the Queen came down to

greet Crumble personally. "Welcome Crumble, I hope you will be very happy here. But from now on you will be called Katherine. Here is your new collar and name tag. You will live with our other Royal Dogs in the cellar. Your training will start tomorrow at 6am sharp." Crumble was devastated.

Where was all the pomp and ceremony and lavish lifestyle? Where was the throne room where she could sit at the feet of the Queen?

This had all gone horribly wrong. And then she thought of Mrs Round and the wonderful times she shared with Alex in the fields and woods.

With heavy legs and a heavy heart Crumble was taken down to the cellars. Life that was so full of promise now looked very bleak.

But Crumble had already made up her mind. She had to escape and get back to Alex.

Chapter 10

A Life on the Run

For three weeks Katherine was trained morning, noon and night. How to bow, how to curtsey and how to keep quiet when told to.

Katherine was being trained with two other dogs, who were not picking up the training as quickly as she was, and so it was even more boring. But they were nice girls and after training they got on well. Bernice and Eunice had a royal look and behaved impeccably.

Katherine asked them. "Aren't you bored with all this hoo-ha?"

"Oh Katherine," they answered. "We have been brought up to serve the family and be present at royal occasions."

Crumble still couldn't get used to being called Katherine and hated it. Each day, whether training or not, Crumble would observe the movements of staff and the routines of the household. This was vital information if she was to make good her escape.

Crumble, Eunice and Bernice became good friends, although Crumble felt they were a bit too posh for her. Crumble confided in them that this was not the life for her and she planned to escape.

"Oh Katherine, you mustn't do that, because we are such good friends. Although you are not a Corgi you have a royal bearing and one day you will be a Princess." Crumble thought of Alex and Mrs Round and Harry the Horse and Jack and cried a little tear.

The next day the girls were given the morning off and were allowed to do their own thing. Without the ever present training and supervision Crumble had the opportunity to do a little exploring. It was just then she saw her chance. The milkman had just finished his delivery and was pulling out of the Palace grounds. Crumble raced across the courtyard and leapt onto the back of the milk float and hid amongst the crates.

The milkman did not notice a thing, and carried on driving past the sentry and out through the main gate. As soon as they got onto the Mall Crumble jumped out and ran into a nearby park. This was more like it, freedom and fresh air.

Crumble now had the problem of trying to find her way home. And she didn't have a clue. She just knew that somehow she had to get back to Alex and her friends.

Without a collar and name tag Crumble was just another stray on the streets and she needed to be careful she did not end up in prison again. Crumble made her way down the Mall, through Trafalgar Square and on to the Embankment. Crossing roads was tricky, but she quickly learnt to wait at the traffic lights with all the other people and cross when they crossed.

The day went quickly and Crumble found it not too difficult to scrounge food and drink from the people she met. But all this walking on concrete was tiring and hurt her soft pads. That night she slept rough in the doorway of a church. It was quiet with not many people around. Early the next day Crumble set off and wandered down street after street with no sign of the farmhouse or Mrs Round. Surely they couldn't be too far away...

Day after day the same routine, sleep in a church doorway, start early, wander through endless streets, cadge food and then back sleeping in a church doorway.

But each day Crumble got weaker and weaker and thinner and thinner. She was running out of energy and her pads were torn and blistered. Her once silky black coat was now dirty and tattered.

As Crumble settled down for yet another night she wondered how much longer she could keep going. Tired, hungry and sore, with her coat crusted in dirt, she realised she could not go any further. She needed to rest and regain her strength and so decided to stay put for a few days.

Crumble liked this church. It was the best one she had found so far and she thought it would be a good place to stay until she felt better. It also had a nice porch where she could sleep at night and get some protection from the cold.

Next day she laid low, and kept herself well hidden in the small but pretty graveyard, determined to spend as many days here as possible. That afternoon a big crowd turned up, and Crumble hid behind a large gravestone so no one could see her. There was much rejoicing and everyone seemed happy, except Crumble that is. Tucked in behind her gravestone she enjoyed the singing and felt safe because no one could see her.

Dozing gently Crumble was suddenly woken by the noise of someone or something approaching. The footsteps were getting nearer. On full alert and ready to run, Crumble was amazed to see a little dog saunter round the gravestone and confront her. Too weak to run or fight Crumble decided that the game was up, back to prison or back to the Palace.

"Hello Crumble, what are you doing here?" It was Jack, the Jack Russell from the vicarage. Relief swept over Crumble and she started to cry. "Oh Jack, I am so pleased to see you but what are you doing here?"

"I'm here with Father Murphy at a special ceremony. But first things first, let's get you some food and drink. You look terrible." Crumble followed Jack into the church hall where some sort of party was going on.

There were huge plates of food and drink and Crumble was made very welcome. Everyone could see what a terrible state she was in and wanted to help. Plates of succulent ham and chicken suddenly appeared and Crumble tucked in with her usual enthusiasm returning. When at last she could eat no more, she explained to Jack what had happened.

Her life in the Palace was just not her and although they treated her well her home was with Alex and Mrs Round. She had escaped and hoped she could find her way home, but after three weeks all she had got was blistered feet, a dirty coat and an empty belly. "But Jack, what are you doing here?"

"Well you know that villain you caught in the church lifting a flagstone and removing a box?"

"Yes I remember," said Crumble, "he was arrested by PC Pipkin."

"Well the thief had discovered the treasure of Eric the Pirate. Everyone thought Eric had buried it in the caves, but he realised that was where everyone would look first. Instead he buried it under a flagstone in the old village church, but died before he could collect his treasure."

"So why the celebration?" asked Crumble. "Father Murphy decided the treasure belonged as much to the village as the church and so everyone will benefit in some way." Crumble was really pleased that with the help of Alex and Charlie and Ollie they had apprehended a thief and helped the village.

Father Murphy was amazed to see Jack with a bedraggled Crumble. He picked her up and was surprised to see how little she weighed.

"Well Crumble, I'm delighted you have found us. We had been told that you had gone missing and we were all praying for your safe return. The Queen has been worried about you and we must get you back to Her Majesty as soon as possible." Despite being weak and feeble Crumble started to struggle to get free and Jack made his feelings known in no uncertain terms. The message was clear, home was with Alex and Mrs Round.

Later that evening Crumble was back in her village. Father Murphy gave her a good bath, a warm meal and a soft bed for the night. For the first time in weeks Crumble enjoyed a deep sleep safe in the knowledge that she was nearly home.

Before anyone was awake, Crumble sneaked out of the vicarage and ran across the fields. Just as she was in sight of her farmhouse, she saw a familiar sight on an early morning explore, Alex!

At the same moment Alex spotted Crumble and they ran like the wind to greet each other. They jumped and shouted with delight and it was just like old times.

"I've missed you Crumble. How long are you staying for?" asked Alex.

"This is where I belong," said Crumble, "and this is where I am going to stay."

Acknowledgements

A special thank you to Maureen Fayle, whose wonderful illustrations have brought each story to life. A lifelong family friend and wonderful artist.

To Crumble and Alex who have brought so much love and fun into our lives, and the inspiration for this book.

To Charlie and Oliver for being the 'rough-and-tumble' boys of all our childhoods.

To my guitar friend Tony, for kind advice and endless proof reading.

To Sheena for introducing me to my publisher.

To the Members of VCP.

And lastly, a very special thank you to Sue and Amanda for their unstinting support and encouragement.

More Author's
From
Violet Circle Publishing

Mike Beale.

Crumble's Adventures.

Children's Fiction.

Discover the wonderful world of Crumble, the little dog with a nose for friends and adventure. This delightful story is an ideal read for young children making their way into advanced reading, and also a wonderful story for mum and dad to read at bedtime.

Robin John Morgan.

Heirs to the Kingdom.

Fantasy Adventure Series.

A fast paced and action packed adventure set in the future after the world is devastated by a deadly virus bringing about the end of modern life as we know it. Join a young boy who has an unnatural talent with a long bow, as he leads a group of his woodland dwelling friends against the might of the powerful Mason Knox. This fantasy adventure takes threads of the past and weaves them into a modern, captivating, and thought provoking tale of the struggle of the woodland people, as they fight to preserve their life at peace within nature.

Ted Morgan.

Wordsmith's Wanderings.

Poetry And Rhymes.

Wordsmith's Wandering is a simple delight to read. Based on the life and observations of the author this reflective and at time very humours collection of poems and rhymes, reflect the 76 years of a man who has served in national service and the health system',whilst working as a member of the Mountain Rescue team.

Find out more about our authors and their books at

www.violetcirclepublishing.co.uk

Violet Circle Publishing, Manchester, UK

www.violetcirclepublishing.co.uk

Lightning Source UK Ltd.
Milton Keynes UK
UKOW01f1247240815

257437UK00001B/12/P